LITTLE M INVENTOR and the ROBOTS

Roger Hargreaves

Original concept by
Roger Hargreaves

Written and illustrated by
Adam Hargreaves

Farshore

C334614087

Little Miss Inventor was always inventing new gadgets to make life easier.

She had a tea-making gadget and a toast-buttering gadget and a breakfast-conveyor gadget that brought her breakfast in bed.

And these were just the gadgets that she had invented for making breakfast.

There were many more.

So many, in fact, that she could hardly move for gadgets!

One morning, while she was waiting in bed for all her gadgets to do their work, she suddenly had a thought.

What you might call a brainwave.

What if she could combine all her gadgets into one machine?

A robot!

After breakfast, she set to work in her workshop at the bottom of her garden.

She welded, and screwed, and calculated, and hammered, and measured, and soldered until she had invented her very first robot.

The HelpBot.

It was a marvel. And it replaced all her other gadgets.

Can you guess who it was inspired by?

The next morning, the HelpBot made tea, and buttered toast, and poured orange juice, and put everything on a tray, and took breakfast up to Little Miss Inventor in bed.

Or it would have done.

But Little Miss Inventor had forgotten one thing.

The staircase!

It was back to the drawing board for Little Miss Inventor.

But it did not take her long to solve the problem.

The HelpBot 2.0 worked like a dream.

The next day, after breakfast in bed, Little Miss Inventor went out for a walk. And as she passed a certain person's house, an extraordinarily long arm reached out of the upstairs window.

I'm sure you can guess who that arm belonged to.

That's right, it was Mr Tickle's! And Mr Tickle's extraordinarily long arm tickled Little Miss Inventor.

"TEE HEE HEE!" she laughed.

Further on, Little Miss Inventor felt a bump on her head.

And then there was a CRASH!

It was Mr Tall.

He was so tall that he had not seen Little Miss Inventor and he had tripped over her!

That evening another thought occurred to Little Miss Inventor.

Mr Tickle's arms could be very useful if they did not tickle you and Mr Tall's legs could be very useful if they did not trip over you.

And so she invented the ExtendaBot!

A robot that could clean gutters, wash upstairs windows and clip tall hedges.

A robot that could feed the giraffe at the zoo!

The next day, while watching Mr Strong help Farmer Field bring in the hay, Little Miss Inventor had another idea for a robot.

The StrongBot.

It was magnificently strong.

It was stupendously strong.

It even helped Mr Funny move house. Literally!

Little Miss Inventor quickly realised that there were all sorts of robots that she could make for all sorts of people.

After tea at Mr Messy's house, she made him a FussyBot inspired by Mr Fussy.

A robot which scrubbed the house until it was as clean as a new pin.

After a failed supper at Mr Lazy's house, she invented the GreedyBot inspired by Mr Greedy.

A robot that was a great chef.

And after waiting for an age for Little Miss Late, she invented the RushBot based on Mr Rush.

A self-drive car that was never late.

Little Miss Inventor was very pleased with all her robots.

However, her friends were not so pleased.

The FussyBot never stopped cleaning.

Mr Messy could not move without it swooping down and cleaning up after him.

He ended up stuck in the corner, unable to move for all the constant cleaning.

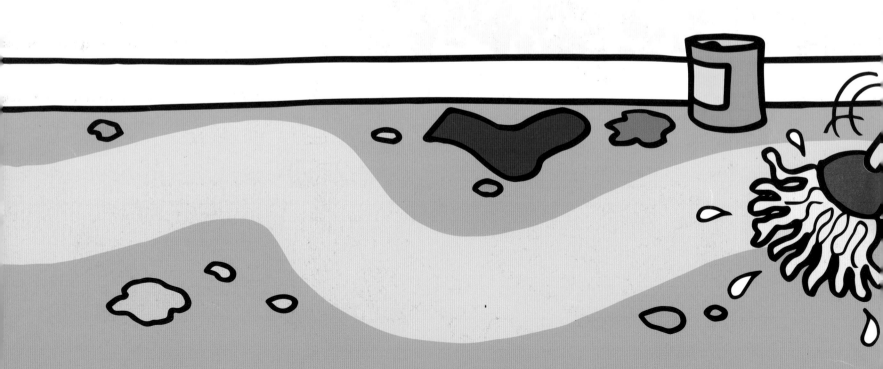

The GreedyBot was an amazing chef.
But it also had an amazing appetite.

It ate everything it cooked!

Poor Mr Lazy.

And the RushBot was always on time, but it was in such a rush to leave that Little Miss Late was always left behind.

And then there were some robots that even
Little Miss Inventor had to admit were a mistake.

Like the ChatterBot.

And the BounceBot.

And the DotBot!

And then she invented the BossyBot.
A robot to take charge.
A robot to ensure that everyone behaved.

And the BossyBot did take charge.

It took charge of Mr Rude.

And Mr Grumpy.

And Little Miss Naughty.

Which was all well and good, but then it went a step too far. Or, more accurately, a wheel too far.

It stopped Mr Funny making jokes.

It stopped Little Miss Hug hugging.

And it stopped Little Miss Giggles giggling.

Then, to make matters even worse, the BossyBot took charge of all Little Miss Inventor's other robots.

A whole team of robots.

The ExtendaBot tied Mr Tickle up in knots.

The BounceBot bounced Mr Bump.

The StrongBot parked Little Miss Sunshine's car in a tree.

The FussyBot tried to vacuum up Little Miss Tiny.

And the GreedyBot ate all the food in town!

It was chaos, the robots had taken over!

Even Little Miss Inventor's HelpBot was far from helpful!

Little Miss Inventor could not believe her eyes.

What had she done?

What could she do?

And then she had an idea.

She hurried down to her shed and invented ...

… a stop button!

And the stop button worked!